Nathaniel Hawthorne

The Pygmies

The Pygmies

Nathaniel Hawthorne

The Pygmies

Nathaniel Hawthorne

A great while ago, when the world was full of wonders, there lived an earth-born Giant, named Antæus, and a million or more of curious little earth-born people, who were called Pygmies. This Giant and these Pygmies being children of the same mother, (that is to say, our good old Grandmother Earth,) were all brethren, and dwelt together in a very friendly and affectionate manner, far, far off, in the middle of hot Africa. The Pygmies were so small, and there were so many sandy deserts and such high mountains between them and the rest of mankind, that nobody could get a peep at them oftener than once in a hundred years. As for the Giant, being of a very lofty stature, it was easy enough to see him, but safest to keep out of his sight.

Among the Pygmies, I suppose, if one of them grew to the height of six or eight inches, he was reckoned a prodigiously tall man. It must have been very pretty to behold their little cities, with streets two or three feet wide, paved with the smallest pebbles, and bordered by habitations about as big as a squirrel's cage. The king's palace attained to the stupendous magnitude of Periwinkle's baby house, and stood in the center of a spacious square, which could hardly have been covered by our hearth rug. Their principal temple, or cathedral, was as lofty as yonder bureau, and was looked upon as a wonderfully sublime and magnificent edifice. All these structures were built neither of stone nor wood. They were neatly plastered together by the Pygmy workmen, pretty much like birds' nests, out of straw, feathers, egg shells, and other small bits of stuff, with stiff clay instead of mortar; and when the hot sun had dried them, they were just as snug and comfortable as a Pygmy could desire.

The country round about was conveniently laid out in fields, the largest of which was nearly of the same extent as one of Sweet Fern's flower beds. Here the Pygmies used to plant wheat and other kinds of grain, which, when it grew up and ripened, overshadowed these tiny people, as the pines, and the oaks, and the walnut and chestnut trees overshadow you and me, when we walk in our own tracts of woodland. At harvest time, they were forced to go with their little axes and cut down the grain, exactly as a woodcutter makes a clearing in the forest; and when a stalk of wheat, with its overburdened top, chanced to come crashing down upon an unfortunate Pygmy, it was apt to be a very sad affair. If it did not smash him all to pieces, at least, I am sure, it must have made the poor little fellow's head ache. And O, my stars! if the fathers and mothers were so small, what must the children and babies have been? A whole family of them might have been put to bed in a shoe, or have crept into an old glove, and played hide and seek in its thumb and fingers. You might have hidden a year-old baby under a thimble.

Now these funny Pygmies, as I told you before, had a Giant for their neighbor and brother, who was bigger, if possible, than they were little. He was so very tall that he carried a pine tree, which was eight feet through the butt, for a walking stick. It took a far-sighted Pygmy, I can assure you, to discern his summit without the help of a telescope; and sometimes, in misty weather, they could not see his upper half, but only his long legs, which seemed to be striding about by themselves. But at noonday, in a clear atmosphere, when the sun shone brightly over him, the Giant Antæus presented a very grand spectacle. There he used to stand, a perfect mountain of a man, with his great countenance smiling down upon his little brothers, and his one vast eye (which was as big as a cart wheel, and placed right in the center of his forehead) giving a friendly wink to the whole nation at once.

The Pygmies loved to talk with Antæus; and fifty times a day, one or another of them would turn up his head, and shout through the hollow of his fists, "Halloo, brother Antæus! How are you, my good fellow?" And when the small, distant squeak of their voices reached his ear, the Giant would make answer, "Pretty well, brother Pygmy, I thank you," in a thunderous roar that would have shaken down the walls of their strongest temple, only that it came from so far aloft.

It was a happy circumstance that Antæus was the Pygmy people's friend; for there was more strength in his little finger than in ten million of such bodies as theirs. If he had been as ill-natured to them as he was to everybody else, he might have beaten down their biggest city at one kick, and hardly have known that he did it. With the tornado of his breath, he could have stripped the roofs from a hundred dwellings, and sent thousands of the inhabitants whirling through the air. He might have set his immense foot upon a multitude; and when he took it up again, there would have been a pitiful sight, to be sure. But, being the son of Mother Earth, as they likewise were, the Giant gave them his brotherly kindness, and loved them with as big a love as it was possible to feel for creatures so very small. And, on their parts, the Pygmies loved Antæus with as much affection as their tiny hearts could hold. He was always ready to do them any good offices that lay in his power; as for example, when they wanted a breeze to turn their wind mills, the Giant would set all the sails a-going with the mere natural respiration of his lungs. When the sun was too hot, he often sat himself down, and let his shadow fall over the kingdom, from one frontier to the other; and as for matters in general, he was wise enough to let them alone, and leave the Pygmies to manage their own affairs—which, after all, is about the best thing that great people can do for little ones.

In short, as I said before, Antæus loved the Pygmies, and the Pygmies loved Antæus. The Giant's life being as long as his body was large, while the lifetime of a Pygmy was but a span, this friendly intercourse had been going on for innumerable generations and ages. It was written about in the Pygmy histories, and talked about in their ancient traditions. The most venerable and white-bearded Pygmy had never heard of a time even, in his greatest of grandfather's days, when the Giant was not their enormous friend. Once, to be sure, (as was recorded on an obelisk, three feet high, erected on the place of the catastrophe,) Antæus sat down upon about five thousand Pygmies who were assembled at a military review. But this was one of those unlucky accidents for which nobody is to blame; so that the small folks never took it to heart and only requested the Giant to be careful forever afterwards to examine the acre of ground where he intended to squat himself.

It is a very pleasant picture to imagine Antæus standing among the Pygmies, like the spire of the tallest cathedral that ever was built, while they ran about like pismires at his feet, and to think that, in spite of their difference in size, there were affection and sympathy between them and him! Indeed, it has always seemed to me that the Giant needed the little people more than the Pygmies needed the Giant. For, unless they had been his neighbors and well wishers, and, as we may say, his playfellows, Antæus would not have had a single friend in the world. No other being like himself had ever been created. No creature of his own size had ever talked with him, in thunder-like accents, face to face. When he stood with his head among the clouds, he was quite alone, and had been so for hundreds of years, and would be so forever. Even if he had met another Giant, Antæus would have fancied the world not big enough for two such vast personages, and, instead of being friends with him, would have fought him till one of the two was killed. But with the Pygmies he was the most sportive, and humorous, and merry-hearted, and sweet-tempered old Giant that ever washed his face in a wet cloud.

His little friends, like all other small people, had a great opinion of their own importance, and used to assume quite a patronizing air towards the giant.

"Poor creature!" they said one to another. "He has a very dull time of it, all by himself; and we ought not to grudge wasting a little of our precious time to amuse him. He is not half so bright as we are, to be sure; and, for that reason, he needs us to look after his comfort and happiness. Let us be kind to the old fellow. Why, if Mother Earth had not been very kind to ourselves, we might all have been Giants too."

On all their holidays, the Pygmies had excellent sport with Antæus. He often stretched himself out at full length on the ground, where he looked like the long ridge of a hill; and it was a good hour's walk, no doubt, for a short-legged Pygmy to journey from head to foot of the Giant. He would lay down his great hand flat on the grass, and challenge the tallest of them to clamber upon it, and straddle from finger to finger. So fearless were they, that they made nothing of creeping in among the folds of his garments. When his head lay sidewise on the earth, they would march boldly up, and peep into the great cavern of his mouth, and take it all as a joke (as indeed it was meant) when Antæus gave a sudden snap with his jaws, as if he were going to swallow fifty of them at once. You would have laughed to see the children dodging in and out among his hair, or swinging from his beard. It is impossible to tell half of the funny tricks that they played with their huge comrade; but I do not know that anything was more curious than when a party of boys were seen running races on his forehead, to try which of them could get first round the circle of his one great eye. It was another favorite feat with them to march along the bridge of his nose, and jump down upon his upper lip.

If the truth must be told, they were sometimes as troublesome to the Giant as a swarm of ants or mosquitoes, especially as they had a fondness for mischief, and liked to prick his skin with their little swords and lances, to see how thick and tough it was. But Antæus took it all kindly enough; although, once in a while, when he happened to be sleepy, he would grumble out a peevish word or two, like the muttering of a tempest, and ask them to have done with their nonsense. A great deal oftener, however, he watched their merriment and gambols until his huge, heavy, clumsy wits were completely stirred up by them; and then would he roar out such a tremendous volume of immeasurable laughter, that the whole nation of Pygmies had to put their hands to their ears, else it would certainly have deafened them.

"Ho! ho! ho!" quoth the Giant, shaking his mountainous sides. "What a funny thing it is to be little! If I were not Antæus, I should like to be a Pygmy, just for the joke's sake."

The Pygmies had but one thing to trouble them in the world. They were constantly at war with the cranes, and had always been so, ever since the long-lived Giant could remember. From time to time, very terrible battles had been fought, in which sometimes the little men won the victory, and sometimes the cranes. According to some historians, the Pygmies used to go to the battle, mounted on the backs of goats and rams; but such animals as these must have been far too big for Pygmies to ride upon; so that, I rather suppose, they rode on squirrelback, or rabbitback, or ratback, or perhaps got upon hedge-hogs, whose prickly quills would be very terrible to the enemy. However this might be, and whatever creatures the Pygmies rode upon, I do not doubt that they made a formidable appearance, armed with sword and spear, and bow and arrow, blowing their tiny trumpet, and shouting their little war cry. They never failed to exhort one another to fight bravely, and recollect that the world had its eyes upon them; although, in simple truth, the only spectator was the Giant Antæus, with his one, great, stupid eye, in the middle of his forehead.

When the two armies joined battle, the cranes would rush forward, flapping their wings and stretching out their necks, and would perhaps snatch up some of the Pygmies crosswise in their beaks. Whenever this happened, it was truly an awful spectacle to see those little men of might kicking and sprawling in the air, and at last disappearing down the crane's long, crooked throat, swallowed up alive. A hero, you know, must hold himself in readiness for any kind of fate; and doubtless the glory of the thing was a consolation to him, even in the crane's gizzard. If Antæus observed that the battle was going hard against his little allies, he generally stopped laughing, and ran with mile-long strides to their assistance, flourishing his club aloft and shouting at the cranes, who quacked and croaked, and retreated as fast as they could. Then the Pygmy army would march homeward in triumph, attributing the victory entirely to their own valor, and to the warlike skill and strategy of whomsoever happened to be captain general; and for a tedious while afterwards, nothing would be heard of but grand processions, and public banquets, and brilliant illuminations, and shows of waxwork, with likenesses of the distinguished officers, as small as life.

In the above-described warfare, if a Pygmy chanced to pluck out a crane's tail feather, it proved a very great feather in his cap. Once or twice, if you will believe me, a little man was made chief ruler of the nation for no other merit in the world than bringing home such a feather.

But I have now said enough to let you see what a gallant little people these were, and how happily they and their forefathers, for nobody knows how many generations, had lived with the immeasurable Giant Antæus. In the remaining part of the story, I shall tell you of a far more astonishing battle than any that was fought between the Pygmies and the cranes.

One day the mighty Antæus was lolling at full length among his little friends. His pine tree walking stick lay on the ground, close by his side. His head was in one part of the kingdom, and his feet extended across the boundaries of another part; and he was taking whatever comfort he could get, while the Pygmies scrambled over him, and peeped into his cavernous mouth, and played among his hair. Sometimes, for a minute or two, the Giant dropped asleep, and snored like the rush of a whirlwind. During one of these little bits of slumber, a Pygmy chanced to climb upon his shoulder, and took a view around the horizon, as from the summit of a hill; and he beheld something, a long way off, which made him rub the bright specks of his eyes, and look sharper than before. At first he mistook it for a mountain, and wondered how it had grown up so suddenly out of the earth. But soon he saw the mountain move. As it came nearer and nearer, what should it turn out to be but a human shape, not so big as Antæus, it is true, although a very enormous figure, in comparison with the Pygmies, and a vast deal bigger than the men whom we see nowadays.

When the Pygmy was quite satisfied that his eyes had not deceived him, he scampered, as fast as his legs would carry him, to the Giant's ear, and stooping over its cavity, shouted lustily into it,—

"Halloo, brother Antæus! Get up this minute, and take your pine tree walking stick in your hand. Here comes another Giant to have a tussle with you."

"Poh, poh!" grumbled Antæus, only half awake. "None of your nonsense, my little fellow! Don't you see I'm sleepy. There is not a Giant on earth for whom I would take the trouble to get up."

But the Pygmy looked again, and now perceived that the stranger was coming directly towards the prostrate form of Antæus. With every step, he looked less like a blue mountain, and more like an immensely large man. He was soon so nigh, that there could be no possible mistake about the matter. There he was, with the sun flaming on his golden helmet, and flashing from his polished breastplate; he had a sword by his side, and a lion's skin over his back, and on his right shoulder he carried a club, which looked bulkier and heavier than the pine-tree walking stick of Antæus.

By this time, the whole nation of Pygmies had seen the new wonder, and a million of them set up a shout, all together; so that it really made quite an audible squeak.

"Get up, Antæus! Bestir yourself, you lazy old Giant! Here comes another Giant, as strong as you are, to fight with you."

"Nonsense, nonsense!" growled the sleepy Giant. "I'll have my nap out, come who may."

Still the stranger drew nearer; and now the Pygmies could plainly discern that, if his stature were less lofty than the Giant's, yet his shoulders were even broader. And, in truth, what a pair of shoulders they must have been! As I told you, a long while ago, they once upheld the sky. The Pygmies, being ten times as vivacious as their great numskull of a brother, could not abide the Giant's slow movements, and were determined to have him on his feet. So they kept shouting to him, and even went so far as to prick him with their swords.

"Get up, get up, get up!" they cried. "Up with you, lazy bones! The strange Giant's club is bigger than your own, his shoulders are the broadest, and we think him the stronger of the two."

Antæus could not endure to have it said that any mortal was half so mighty as himself. This latter remark of the Pygmies pricked him deeper than their swords, and, sitting up, in rather a sulky humor, he gave a gape of several yards wide, rubbed his eye, and finally turned his stupid head in the direction whither his little friends were eagerly pointing.

No sooner did he set his eye on the stranger, than, leaping on his feet, and seizing his walking stick, he strode a mile or two to meet him; all the while brandishing the sturdy pine tree, so that it whistled through the air.

"Who are you?" thundered the Giant. "And what do you want in my dominions?"

There was one strange thing about Antæus, of which I have not yet told you, lest, hearing of so many wonders all in a lump, you might not believe much more than half of them. You are to know, then, that whenever this redoubtable Giant touched the ground, either with his hand, his foot, or any other part of his body, he grew stronger than ever he had been before. The Earth, you remember, was his mother, and was very fond of him, as being almost the biggest of her children; and so she took this method of keeping him always in full vigor. Some persons affirm that he grew ten times stronger at every touch; others say that it was only twice as strong. But only think of it! Whenever Antæus took a walk, supposing it were but ten miles, and that he stepped a hundred yards at a stride, you may try to cipher out how much mightier he was, on sitting down again, than when he first started. And whenever he flung himself on the earth to take a little repose, even if he got up the very next instant, he would be as strong as exactly ten just such Giants as his former self. It was well for the world that Antæus happened to be of a sluggish disposition, and liked ease better than exercise; for, if he had frisked about like the Pygmies, and touched the earth as often as they did, he would long ago have been strong enough to pull down the sky about people's ears. But these great lubberly fellows resemble mountains, not only in bulk, but in their disinclination to move.

Any other mortal man, except the very one whom Antæus had now encountered, would have been half frightened to death by the Giant's ferocious aspect and terrible voice. But the stranger did not seem at all disturbed. He carelessly lifted his club, and balanced it in his hand measuring Antæus with his eye, from head to foot, not as if wonder-smitten at his stature, but as if he had seen a great many Giants before, and this was by no means the biggest of them. In fact, if the Giant had been no bigger than the Pygmies, (who stood pricking up their ears, and looking and listening to what was going forward,) the stranger could not have been less afraid of him.

"Who are you, I say?" roared Antæus again. "What's your name? Why do you come hither? Speak, you vagabond, or I'll try the thickness of your skull with my walking stick."

"You are a very discourteous Giant," answered the stranger, quietly, "and I shall probably have to teach you a little civility, before we part. As for my name, it is Hercules. I have come hither because this is my most convenient road to the garden of the Hesperides, whither I am going to get three of the golden apples for King Eurystheus."

"Caitiff, you shall go no farther!" bellowed Antæus, putting on a grimmer look than before; for he had heard of the mighty Hercules, and hated him because he was said to be so strong. "Neither shall you go back whence you came!"

"How will you prevent me," asked Hercules, "from going whither I please?"

"By hitting you a rap with this pine tree here," shouted Antæus, scowling so that he made himself the ugliest monster in Africa. "I am fifty times stronger than you; and, now that I stamp my foot upon the ground, I am five hundred times stronger! I am ashamed to kill such a puny little dwarf as you seem to be. I will make a slave of you, and you shall likewise be the slave of my brethren, here, the Pygmies. So throw down your club and your other weapons; and as for that lion's skin, I intend to have a pair of gloves made of it."

"Come and take it off my shoulders, then," answered Hercules, lifting his club.

Then the Giant, grinning with rage, strode tower-like towards the stranger, (ten times strengthened at every step,) and fetched a monstrous blow at him with his pine tree, which Hercules caught upon his club; and being more skilful than Antæus, he paid him back such a rap upon the sconce, that down tumbled the great lumbering man-mountain, flat upon the ground. The poor little Pygmies (who really never dreamed that anybody in the world was half so strong as their brother Antæus) were a good deal dismayed at this. But no sooner was the Giant down, than up he bounced again, with tenfold might, and such a furious visage as was horrible to behold. He aimed another blow at Hercules, but struck awry, being blinded with wrath, and only hit his poor innocent Mother Earth, who groaned and trembled at the stroke. His pine tree went so deep into the ground, and stuck there so fast, that, before Antæus could get it out, Hercules brought down his club across his shoulders with a mighty thwack, which made the Giant roar as if all sorts of intolerable noises had come screeching and rumbling out of his immeasurable lungs in that one cry. Away it went, over mountains and valleys, and, for aught I know, was heard on the other side of the African deserts.

As for the Pygmies, their capital city was laid in ruins by the concussion and vibration of the air; and, though there was uproar enough without their help, they all set up a shriek out of three millions of little throats, fancying, no doubt, that they swelled the Giant's bellow by at least ten times as much. Meanwhile, Antæus had scrambled upon his feet again, and pulled his pine tree out of the earth; and, all aflame with fury, and more outrageously strong than ever, he ran at Hercules, and brought down another blow.

"This time, rascal, shouted he, you shall not escape me."

But once more Hercules warded off the stroke with his club, and the Giant's pine tree was shattered into a thousand splinters, most of which flew among the Pygmies, and did them more mischief than I like to think about. Before Antæus could get out of the way, Hercules let drive again, and gave him another knock-down blow, which sent him heels over head, but served only to increase his already enormous and insufferable strength. As for his rage, there is no telling what a fiery furnace it had now got to be. His one eye was nothing but a circle of red flame. Having now no weapons but his fists, he doubled them up, (each bigger than a hogshead,) smote one against the other, and danced up and down with absolute frenzy, flourishing his immense arms about, as if he meant not merely to kill Hercules, but to smash the whole world to pieces.

"Come on!" roared this thundering Giant. "Let me hit you but one box on the ear, and you'll never have the headache again."

Now Hercules (though strong enough, as you already know, to hold the sky up) began to be sensible that he should never win the victory, if he kept on knocking Antæus down; for, by and by, if he hit him such hard blows, the Giant would inevitably, by the help of his Mother Earth, become stronger than the mighty Hercules himself. So, throwing down his club, with which he had fought so many dreadful battles, the hero stood ready to receive his antagonist with naked arms.

"Step forward," cried he. "Since I've broken your pine tree, we'll try which is the better man at a wrestling match."

"Aha! then I'll soon satisfy you," shouted the Giant; for, if there was one thing on which he prided himself more than another, it was his skill in wrestling. "Villain, I'll fling you where you can never pick yourself up again."

On came Antæus, hopping and capering with the scorching heat of his rage, and getting new vigor wherewith to wreak his passion, every time he hopped. But Hercules, you must understand, was wiser than this numskull of a Giant, and had thought of a way to fight him,—huge, earth-born monster that he was,—and to conquer him too, in spite of all that his Mother Earth could do for him. Watching his opportunity, as the mad Giant made a rush at him, Hercules caught him round the middle with both hands, lifted him high into the air, and held him aloft overhead.

Just imagine it, my dear little friends! What a spectacle it must have been, to see this monstrous fellow sprawling in the air, face downward, kicking out his long legs and wriggling his whole vast body, like a baby when its father holds it at arm's length towards the ceiling.

But the most wonderful thing was, that, as soon as Antæus was fairly off the earth, he began to lose the vigor which he had gained by touching it. Hercules very soon perceived that his troublesome enemy was growing weaker, both because he struggled and kicked with less violence, and because the thunder of his big voice subsided into a grumble. The truth was, that, unless the Giant touched Mother Earth as often as once in five minutes, not only his overgrown strength, but the very breath of his life, would depart from him. Hercules had guessed this secret; and it may be well for us all to remember it, in case we should ever have to fight a battle with a fellow like Antæus. For these earth-born creatures are only difficult to conquer on their own ground, but may be managed if we can contrive to lift them into a loftier and purer region. So it proved with the poor Giant, whom I am really a little sorry for, notwithstanding his uncivil way of treating strangers who came to visit him.

When his strength and breath were quite gone, Hercules gave his huge body a toss, and flung it about a mile off, where it fell heavily, and lay with no more motion than a sand hill. It was too late for the Giant's Mother Earth to help him now; and I should not wonder if his ponderous bones were lying on the same spot to this very day, and were mistaken for those of an uncommonly large elephant.

But, alas me! What a wailing did the poor little Pygmies set up when they saw their enormous brother treated in this terrible manner. If Hercules heard their shrieks, however, he took no notice, and perhaps fancied them only the shrill, plaintive twittering of small birds that had been frightened from their nests by the uproar of the battle between himself and Antæus. Indeed, his thoughts had been so much taken up with the Giant, that he had never once looked at the Pygmies, nor even knew that there was such a funny little nation in the world. And now, as he had travelled a good way, and was also rather weary with his exertions in the fight, he spread out his lion's skin on the ground, and reclining himself upon it, fell fast asleep.

As soon as the Pygmies saw Hercules preparing for a nap, they nodded their little heads at one another, and winked with their little eyes. And when his deep, regular breathing gave them notice that he was asleep, they assembled together in an immense crowd, spreading over a space of about twenty-seven feet square. One of their most eloquent orators (and a valiant warrior enough, besides, though hardly so good at any other weapon as he was with his tongue) climbed upon a toadstool, and, from that elevated position, addressed the multitude. His sentiments were pretty much as follows; or, at all events, something like this was probably the upshot of his speech:—

"Tall Pygmies and mighty little men! You and all of us have seen what a public calamity has been brought to pass, and what an insult has here been offered to the majesty of our nation. Yonder lies Antæus, our great friend and brother, slain, within our territory, by a miscreant who took him at disadvantage, and fought him (if fighting it can be called) in a way that neither man, nor Giant, nor Pygmy ever dreamed of fighting, until this hour. And, adding a grievous contumely to the wrong already done us, the miscreant has now fallen asleep as quietly as if nothing were to be dreaded from our wrath! It behooves you, fellow-countrymen, to consider in what aspect we shall stand before the world, and what will be the verdict of impartial history, should we suffer these accumulated outrages to go unavenged.

"Antæus was our brother, born of that same beloved parent to whom we owe the thews and sinews, as well as the courageous hearts, which made him proud of our relationship. He was our faithful ally, and fell fighting as much for our national rights and immunities as for his own personal ones. We and our forefathers have dwelt in friendship with him, and held affectionate intercourse, as man to man, through immemorial generations. You remember how often our entire people have reposed in his great shadow, and how our little ones have played at hide and seek in the tangles of his hair, and how his mighty footsteps have familiarly gone to and fro among us, and never trodden upon any of our toes. And there lies this dear brother—this sweet and amiable friend—this brave and faithful ally—this virtuous Giant—this blameless and excellent Antæus—dead! Dead. Silent! Powerless! A mere mountain of clay! Forgive my tears! Nay, I behold your own. Were we to drown the world with them, could the world blame us?

"But to resume: Shall we, my countrymen, suffer this wicked stranger to depart unharmed, and triumph in his treacherous victory, among distant communities of the earth? Shall we not rather compel him to leave his bones here on our soil, by the side of our slain brother's bones? So that, while one skeleton shall remain as the everlasting monument of our sorrow, the other shall endure as long, exhibiting to the whole human race a terrible example of Pygmy vengeance! Such is the question. I put it to you in full confidence of a response that shall be worthy of our national character, and calculated to increase, rather than diminish, the glory which our ancestors have transmitted to us, and which we ourselves have proudly vindicated in our warfare with the cranes."

The orator was here interrupted by a burst of irrepressible enthusiasm; every individual Pygmy crying out that the national honor must be preserved at all hazards. He bowed, and making a gesture for silence, wound up his harangue in the following admirable manner:—

"It only remains for us, then, to decide whether we shall carry on the war in our national capacity,—one united people against a common enemy,—or whether some champion, famous in former fights, shall be selected to defy the slayer of our brother Antæus to single combat. In the latter case, though not unconscious that there may be taller men among you, I hereby offer myself for that enviable duty. And, believe me, dear countrymen, whether I live or die, the honor of this great country, and the fame bequeathed us by our heroic progenitors, shall suffer no diminution in my hands. Never, while I can wield this sword, of which I now fling away the scabbard—never, never, never, even if the crimson hand that slew the great Antæus shall lay me prostrate, like him, on the soil which I give my life to defend."

So saying, this valiant Pygmy drew out his weapon, (which was terrible to behold, being as long as the blade of a penknife,) and sent the scabbard whirling over the heads of the multitude. His speech was followed by an uproar of applause, as its patriotism and self-devotion unquestionably deserved; and the shouts and clapping of hands would have been greatly prolonged, had they not been rendered quite inaudible by a deep respiration, vulgarly called a snore, from the sleeping Hercules.

It was finally decided that the whole nation of Pygmies should set to work to destroy Hercules; not, be it understood, from any doubt that a single champion would be capable of putting him to the sword, but because he was a public enemy, and all were desirous of sharing in the glory of his defeat. There was a debate whether the national honor did not demand that a herald should be sent with a trumpet, to stand over the ear of Hercules, and, after blowing a blast right into it, to defy him to the combat by formal proclamation. But two or three venerable and sagacious Pygmies, well versed in state affairs, gave it as their opinion that war already existed, and that it was their rightful privilege to take the enemy by surprise. Moreover if awakened, and allowed to get upon his feet, Hercules might happen to do them a mischief before he could be beaten down again. For, as these sage counsellers remarked, the stranger's club was really very big, and had rattled like a thunderbolt against the skull of Antæus. So the Pygmies resolved to set aside all foolish punctilios, and assail their antagonist at once.

Accordingly, all the fighting men of the nation took their weapons, and went boldly up to Hercules, who still lay fast asleep, little dreaming of the harm which the Pygmies meant to do him. A body of twenty thousand archers marched in front, with their little bows all ready, and the arrows on the string. The same number were ordered to clamber upon Hercules, some with spades, to dig his eyes out, and others with bundles of hay, and all manner of rubbish, with which they intended to plug up his mouth and nostrils, so that he might perish for lack of breath. These last, however, could by no means perform their appointed duty; inasmuch as the enemy's breath rushed out of his nose in an obstreperous hurricane and whirlwind, which blew the Pygmies away as fast as they came nigh. It was found necessary, therefore, to hit upon some other method of carrying on the war.

After holding a council, the captains ordered their troops to collect sticks, straws, dry weeds, and whatever combustible stuff they could find and make a pile of it, heaping it high around the head of Hercules. As a great many thousand Pygmies were employed in this task, they soon brought together several bushels of inflammatory matter, and raised so tall a heap, that, mounting on its summit, they were quite upon a level with the sleeper's face. The archers, meanwhile, were stationed within bow shot, with orders to let fly at Hercules the instant that he stirred. Everything being in readiness, a torch was applied to the pile, which immediately burst into flames, and soon waxed hot enough to roast the enemy, had he but chosen to lie still. A Pygmy, you know, though so very small, might set the world on fire, just as easily as a Giant could; so that this was certainly the very best way of dealing with their foe, provided they could have kept him quiet while the conflagration was going forward.

But no sooner did Hercules begin to be scorched, than up he started, with his hair in a red blaze.

"What's all this?" he cried, bewildered with sleep, and staring about him as if he expected to see another Giant.

At that moment the twenty thousand archers twanged their bowstrings, and the arrows came whizzing, like so many winged mosquitoes, right into the face of Hercules. But I doubt whether more than half a dozen of them punctured the skin, which was remarkably tough, as you know the skin of a hero has good need to be.

"Villain!" shouted all the Pygmies at once. "You have killed the Giant Antæus, our great brother, and the ally of our nation. We declare bloody war against you, and will slay you on the spot."

Surprised at the shrill piping of so many little voices, Hercules, after putting out the conflagration of his hair, gazed all round about, but could see nothing. At last, however, looking narrowly on the ground, he espied the innumerable assemblage of Pygmies at his feet. He stooped down, and taking up the nearest one between his thumb and finger, set him on the palm of his left hand, and held him at a proper distance for examination. It chanced to be the very identical Pygmy who had spoken from the top of the toadstool, and had offered himself as a champion to meet Hercules in single combat.

"What in the world, my little fellow," ejaculated Hercules, "may you be?"

"I am your enemy," answered the valiant Pygmy, in his mightiest squeak.

"You have slain the enormous Antæus, our brother by the mother's side, and for ages the faithful ally of our illustrious nation. We are determined to put you to death; and for my own part, I challenge you to instant battle, on equal ground."

Hercules was so tickled with the Pygmy's big words and warlike gestures, that he burst into a great explosion of laughter, and almost dropped the poor little mite of a creature off the palm of his hand, through the ecstasy and convulsion of his merriment.

"Upon my word," cried he, "I thought I had seen wonders before to-day—hydras with nine heads, stags with golden horns, six-legged men, three-headed dogs, giants with furnaces in their stomachs, and nobody knows what besides. But here, on the palm of my hand, stands a wonder that outdoes them all! Your body, my little friend, is about the size of an ordinary man's finger: Pray, how big may your soul be?"

"As big as your own!" said the Pygmy.

Hercules was touched with the little man's dauntless courage, and could not help acknowledging such a brotherhood with him as one hero feels for another.

"My good little people," said he, making a low obeisance to the grand nation, "not for all the world would I do an intentional injury to such brave fellows as you! Your hearts seem to me so exceedingly great, that, upon my honor, I marvel how your small bodies can contain them. I sue for peace, and, as a condition of it, will take five strides, and be out of your kingdom at the sixth. Good-by. I shall pick my steps carefully, for fear of treading upon some fifty of you, without knowing it. Ha, ha, ha! Ho, ho, ho! For once, Hercules acknowledges himself vanquished."

Some writers say, that Hercules gathered up the whole race of Pygmies in his lion's skin, and carried them home to Greece, for the children of King Eurystheus to play with. But this is a mistake. He left them, one and all, within their own territory, where, for aught I can tell, their descendants are alive to the present day, building their little houses, cultivating their little fields, spanking their little children, waging their little warfare with the cranes, doing their little business, whatever it may be, and reading their little histories of ancient times. In those histories, perhaps, it stands recorded, that, a great many centuries ago, the valiant Pygmies avenged the death of the Giant Antæus by scaring away the mighty Hercules.

20

"You have slain the enormous Antæus, our brother by the mother's side, and for ages the faithful ally of our illustrious nation. We are determined to put you to death; and for my own part, I challenge you to instant battle, on equal ground."

Hercules was so tickled with the Pygmy's big words and warlike gestures, that he burst into a great explosion of laughter, and almost dropped the poor little mite of a creature off the palm of his hand, through the ecstasy and convulsion of his merriment.

"Upon my word," cried he, "I thought I had seen wonders before to-day—hydras with nine heads, stags with golden horns, six-legged men, three-headed dogs, giants with furnaces in their stomachs, and nobody knows what besides. But here, on the palm of my hand, stands a wonder that outdoes them all! Your body, my little friend, is about the size of an ordinary man's finger. Pray, how big may your soul be?"

"As big as your own!" said the Pygmy.

Hercules was touched with the little man's dauntless courage, and could not help acknowledging such a brotherhood with him as one hero feels for another.

"My good little people," said he, making a low obeisance to the grand nation, "not for all the world would I do an intentional injury to such brave fellows as you! Your hearts seem to me so exceedingly great, that, upon my honor, I marvel how your small bodies can contain them. I sue for peace, and, as a condition of it, will take five strides, and be out of your kingdom at the sixth. Good-by. I shall pick my steps carefully, for fear of treading upon some fifty of you, without knowing it. Ha, ha, ha! Ho, ho, ho! For once, Hercules acknowledges himself vanquished."

Some writers say, that Hercules gathered up the whole race of Pygmies in his lion's skin, and carried them home to Greece, for the children of King Eurystheus to play with. But this is a mistake. He left them, one and all, within their own territory, where, for aught I can tell, their descendants are alive to the present day, building their little houses, cultivating their little fields, spanking their little children, waging their little warfare with the cranes, doing their little business, whatever it may be, and reading their little histories of ancient times. In those histories, perhaps, it stands recorded, that, a great many centuries ago, the valiant Pygmies avenged the death of the Giant Antæus by scaring away the mighty Hercules.

"You have slain the enormous Antæus, our brother by the mother's side, and for ages the faithful ally of our illustrious nation. We are determined to put you to death; and for my own part, I challenge you to instant battle, on equal ground."

Hercules was so tickled with the Pygmy's big words and warlike gestures, that he burst into a great explosion of laughter, and almost dropped the poor little mite of a creature off the palm of his hand, through the ecstasy and convulsion of his merriment.

"Upon my word," cried he, "I thought I had seen wonders before to-day—hydras with nine heads, stags with golden horns, six-legged men, three-headed dogs, giants with furnaces in their stomachs, and nobody knows what besides. But here, on the palm of my hand, stands a wonder that outdoes them all! Your body, my little friend, is about the size of an ordinary man's finger. Pray, how big may your soul be?"

"As big as your own!" said the Pygmy.

Hercules was touched with the little man's dauntless courage, and could not help acknowledging such a brotherhood with him as one hero feels for another.

"My good little people," said he, making a low obeisance to the grand nation, "not for all the world would I do an intentional injury to such brave fellows as you! Your hearts seem to me so exceedingly great, that, upon my honor, I marvel how your small bodies can contain them. I sue for peace, and, as a condition of it, will take five strides, and be out of your kingdom at the sixth. Good-by. I shall pick my steps carefully, for fear of treading upon some fifty of you, without knowing it. Ha, ha, ha! Ho, ho, ho! For once, Hercules acknowledges himself vanquished."

Some writers say, that Hercules gathered up the whole race of Pygmies in his lion's skin, and carried them home to Greece, for the children of King Eurystheus to play with. But this is a mistake. He left them, one and all, within their own territory, where, for aught I can tell, their descendants are alive to the present day, building their little houses, cultivating their little fields, spanking their little children, waging their little warfare with the cranes, doing their little business, whatever it may be, and reading their little histories of ancient times. In those histories, perhaps, it stands recorded, that, a great many centuries ago, the valiant Pygmies avenged the death of the Giant Antæus by scaring away the mighty Hercules.